D0771256

TREASURY OF

Bedtime Stories

Cover illustrated by Simon Taylor-Kielty

Louis Weber, C.E.O., Publications International, Ltd.
7373 North Cicero Avenue, Lincolnwood, Illinois 60712

Ground Floor, 59 Gloucester Place, London W1U 8JJ

Customer Service: 1-800-595-8484 or customer_service@pilbooks.com

www.pilbooks.com

8 7 6 5 4 3 2 1

Manufactured in China.

ISBN-10: 1-4508-2410-2
ISBN-13: 978-1-4508-2410-1

TREASURY OF
Bedtime Stories

pi kids® publications international, ltd.

Table of Contents

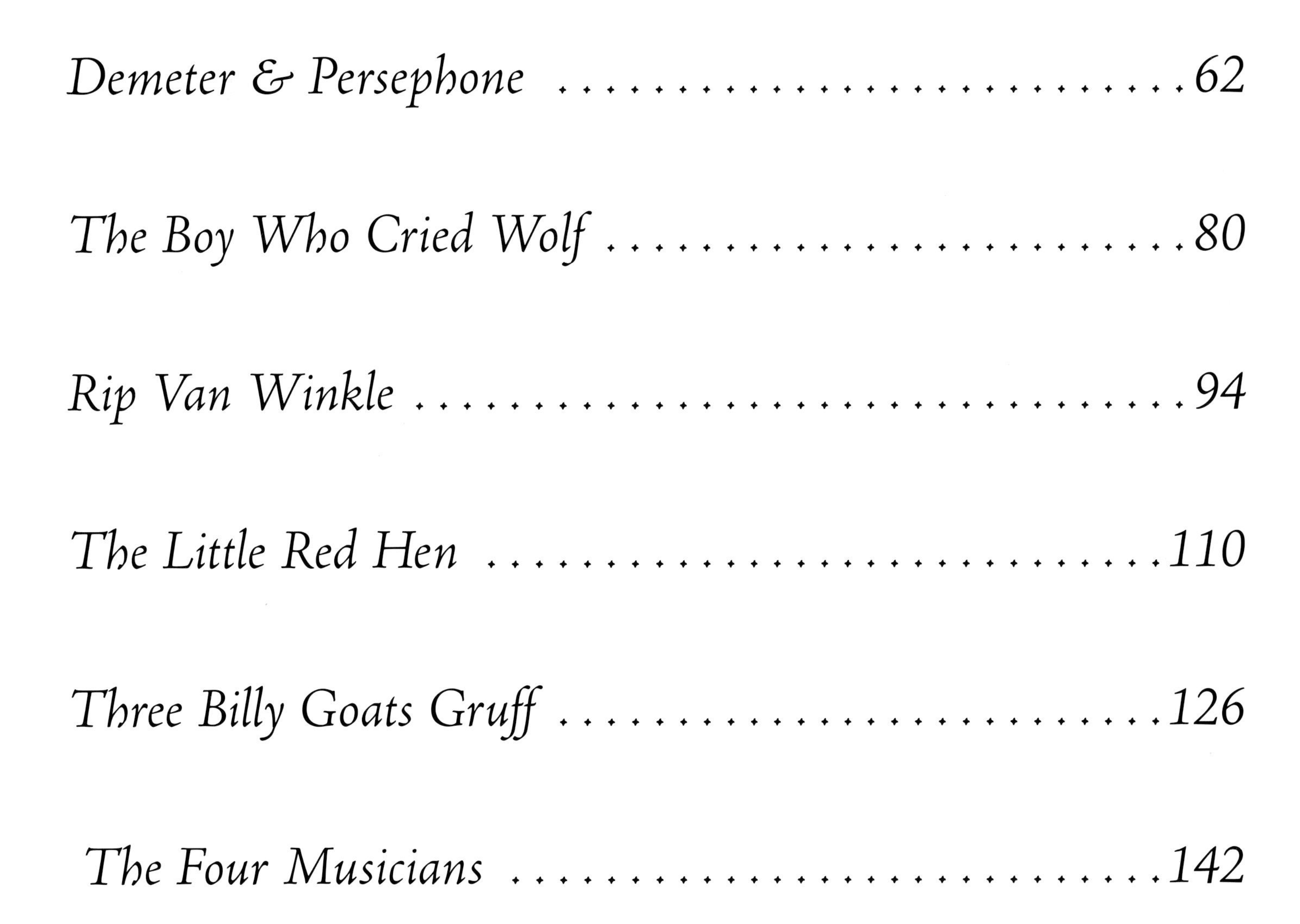

Little Red Riding Hood

Adapted by Lawrence A. West
Illustrated by Thea Kliros

In a small town next to a large forest, there lived a little girl. She was called Little Red Riding Hood.

One day her mother said, "Grandma is sick. Please take her this basket of goodies. Be careful and be sure to stay on the path."

"All right, Mother," said Little Red Riding Hood, as she walked off with the basket.

Little Red Riding Hood soon forgot her mother's warning. She wandered off the path and soon met a wolf.

"Where are you going, little girl?" asked the wolf. "What do you have in that basket?"

"I am going to visit my grandmother, who lives in the house with the red door," answered the girl. "She's sick, and I'm taking her a basket of treats."

"Do you have any fresh strawberries in your basket?" asked the wolf.

"No," admitted Red Riding Hood.

"Surely your grandmother would like some," said the wolf. "My grandmother loves strawberries."

Little Red Riding Hood said, "Grandma does love strawberries. I'll run and pick some right now for her."

"You can leave your basket with me," suggested the hungry wolf. "I'd be happy to watch it for you."

"No, thank you," said Little Red Riding Hood. "I'll bring it with me, so I can carry the strawberries."

The disappointed wolf watched Little Red Riding Hood hurry away. He was very hungry, and a basket of goodies sounded delicious.

The wolf sat and licked his lips. He needed to come up with another plan. He picked a bouquet of flowers and waited for Little Red Riding Hood to come back.

Later, she came skipping towards the wolf.

"I see that you do not have any flowers for your grandmother," said the wolf. "I have just picked this bouquet for my own grandmother. I suggest you pick one, too. I know your grandmother would like it."

"Grandmother does love flowers," said Little Red Riding Hood. And she began to search for the loveliest yellow and white blooms she could find. She was so busy picking flowers that she did not see the wolf run off in the direction of Grandma's house.

Little Red Riding Hood gathered her flowers and skipped off to deliver her gifts.

At the same time, the wolf sneaked into Grandmother's house. He frightened her so greatly that she ran out the front door!

Then the wolf dressed in one of Grandmother's nightgowns. He put on a sleeping bonnet and slipped into Grandmother's comfortable bed, where he waited for Little Red Riding Hood.

The wolf hadn't been waiting long when he heard the front door open.

"Hello, Grandmother," called Little Red Riding Hood.

"Hello, dear," said the wolf in a disguised voice. "Please come in. I am resting in bed."

Red Riding Hood walked into Grandmother's room.

"I hope you're feeling better, Grandmother," she said. "I brought you a basket of goodies from Mother and me."

"Thank you, my dear," said the wolf. "That is very kind. Your basket of goodies certainly smells delicious. Please, come closer, and give me some news from the village."

Little Red Riding Hood stepped closer to the bed. Her grandmother looked very strange! She was surprised to see that her grandmother's eyes looked so large.

"Why, Grandmother," said Little Red Riding Hood, "what big eyes you have!"

The wolf blinked, trying to hide them from her.

"All the better to see you with, my dear," he said.

As the wolf shifted in the bed to hide his eyes, the bonnet slipped from his head.

"Why, Grandmother," said Little Red Riding Hood, "what big ears you have!"

"All the better to hear you with, my dear," the wolf replied, as he fixed the bonnet on his head. When the wolf fixed the bonnet, the covers slipped from his face.

"Why, Grandmother," said Little Red Riding Hood, "what big teeth you have!"

"All the better to EAT you with!" cried the wolf.

With that, Little Red Riding Hood let out a scream and ran from the room. The wolf leaped from the bed and chased after her.

When the wolf reached out to grab her cape, she knocked over a chair and ran away.

"Stop!" cried a loud voice, suddenly. Little Red Riding Hood looked back to see a woodcutter.

The woodcutter held an ax in the air.

"Do you think you scare me?" asked the wolf.

"I believe I should," said the woodcutter. The wolf went to run after Little Red Riding Hood again. But the woodcutter grabbed the wolf by the tail and carried him into the forest. Little Red Riding Hood was safe.

Grandmother came running up to Little Red Riding Hood. She had been hiding nearby, in the garden shed.

"I'm so glad you're safe," cried Little Red Riding Hood. "I was worried that the wolf had eaten you!"

Grandmother gave Little Red Riding Hood a great big hug as the woodcutter came out of the woods.

"I don't think that wolf will trouble you again," he said, adjusting his cap.

"Thank you very much," said Grandmother. "Won't you please join us for a snack?"

"I would enjoy that very much," said the woodcutter.

Together, the three of them enjoyed the basket of goodies as they sat and told stories for the rest of the day.

As the woodcutter had promised, Little Red Riding Hood never saw the wolf again. Just to be sure, Little Red Riding Hood always stayed on the path when walking to Grandmother's house.

The City Mouse & The Country Mouse

Adapted by Lisa Harkrader
Illustrated by Dominic Catalano

Once upon a time a country mouse named Oliver lived in a hole under the root of a big oak tree. Oliver loved his home in the forest surrounded by chattering squirrels, chirping crickets, and hearty plants.

One day Oliver decided to invite his city cousin, Alistair, for a visit. Before Alistair arrived, Oliver tidied up his house. He straightened the leaves on his bed, placed fresh pine needles on the floor, polished his plates, and dusted his table.

Then Oliver sat by his door and gazed out at the quiet stars to wait for his cousin.

"Alistair will surely like it here," Oliver said to himself.

When Alistair arrived, he set his fine leather suitcase on Oliver's rug of fresh pine needles.

"Oliver, is this your cellar?" he asked.

"No, it's my home," said Oliver, as he sat his cousin down at the table and served him a dinner of barley, wheat, and dandelion tea.

Alistair nibbled his meal politely. "This tastes as though it's good for me, although it doesn't have much flavor!" he chuckled to himself.

After dinner they both settled into their beds and went to sleep. The next morning, a robin family twittered in the oak tree and a rooster crowed at a nearby farm. Oliver leapt from his bed to start his day.

"I love to hear the sounds of the countryside early in the morning," said Oliver. "It makes me want to jump out of bed to start my day."

"You start your day this early?" asked Alistair.

"I can't stand that confounded racket," said Alistair as he pressed his pillow to his ears and tried to fall back asleep.

Oliver put on his overalls, pulled up his work boots, and pushed his wheelbarrow out into the sunshine to begin his day. Alistair yawned and rolled out of bed.

When he stumbled outside into the sunshine, he thought it was much too bright for his eyes and much too hot to do any work.

"How can you possibly work in this weather?" asked Alistair as he sat in the shade.

"What do you mean?" asked Oliver. "The weather out here is beautiful!" Oliver shucked seeds from tall rye grass and set them out to dry. Alistair continued to watch Oliver from underneath the shade of a tree. Alistair watched his cousin collect acorns, corn husks, and water.

"There! This work is done," said Oliver.

"Thank goodness," said Alistair.

CITY

Alistair used his handkerchief to wipe the dust from his shiny shoes. "I think it's high time for a snack and a nap, don't you?" he asked Oliver.

Oliver giggled. "All of my work isn't finished. I still have to carry in water and trim the roots growing in my kitchen."

Alistair sighed. "I'm simply not cut out for country life," he said. "You work too hard for your dinner here, and all you end up with is a pile of seeds! Come back to the city with me, and I'll show you the good life."

So the two mice set out for Alistair's home in the city. Oliver followed Alistair over fields and valleys, into subway tunnels, and across crowded city parks until they arrived on Alistair's street.

Alistair stopped in front of a beautiful hotel. "Welcome to my home! This is how mice should really live," he said.

Oliver stared up at the revolving glass door. "But how do we get in?" he asked.

"We wait until it turns, and then we run through as fast as we can!" said Alistair.

When the door started to turn, Alistair darted inside. A frightened Oliver gathered his courage and dove inside after Alistair. He tried to follow his cousin, but his bag became caught on the door. Oliver went round and round so many times, he couldn't tell whether he was right side up or upside down!

Finally, Alistair pulled him out of the doors and led Oliver across a beautiful marble hallway to a small crack hidden by heavy velvet drapes. "Here is my apartment!" Alistair announced.

Oliver looked around in amazement. There were so many fancy things everywhere! Alistair showed Oliver around his apartment.

"We're under the bandstand," Alistair told him. "An orchestra plays every night and people dance till morning."

Hotel
DeLuxury

DeLuxury

"How can you sleep with all that noise?" asked Oliver.

"Sleep?" asked Alistair. "I sleep when I want! I never have to worry about being up early."

Alistair led Oliver through the hotel and into the dining room. They hid behind plants and raced under tablecloths until they arrived in the chef's kitchen.

"You don't want anyone to see you," warned Alistair, "or worse, catch you."

Oliver was nervous. Where was Alistair taking him? What would happen to them if they were seen or caught?

"Do be careful," Alistair warned again as he quickly and quietly opened the pantry door. Inside the pantry Oliver saw shelf after shelf of cheeses, jams, fruit, and meat.

The two mice entered the pantry and Oliver followed his cousin up the shelves. "Now this is fine dining!" Alistair announced as he crunched into a cracker. "Please help yourself, cousin, to anything you would like."

Alistair hopped up to the top shelf of the pantry and sat down to fill his stomach with pretzels, crackers, cheese, and olives.

Oliver was hungry, too, but he was so nervous he could not eat a crumb.

"Tonight the chef is preparing his signature roast duck with herbed potatoes in a cream sauce," said Alistair. "One taste of that and you'll never want to go back to the country! Follow me, it's time for the main course! Our chef is quite a messy fellow," said Alistair. "He drops chunks of meat and potatoes and dollops of sauce all over the floor. One time I found an entire turkey leg under the stove. That was quite a feast."

Alistair darted around the floor picking up bits of duck and potatoes. He didn't notice the chef walking back into the kitchen.

"You again!" shouted the chef.

"And this time you've brought a friend?" asked the chef. "I will not have you furry little pests in my five-star kitchen!" The chef took a broom and chased the mice around the kitchen until Alistair and Oliver escaped through a hole under the sink.

"No main course tonight!" said Alistair. "We'll have to make up for it with dessert."

Alistair led Oliver into the dining room where they settled beneath a pastry cart. Alistair feasted on pies and pastry, but Oliver lost his balance and fell straight into a cream puff.

The mice rode the dessert cart until it stopped next to Alistair's apartment. Oliver wobbled off the cart and ran into Alistair's apartment before anyone could catch them.

"You take too many risks for your supper," said Oliver. "A mouse could starve to death here. There is plenty of delicious food, but I'm too frightened to eat it!"

"Perhaps you are not cut out for the city, just like I'm not cut out for the country," Alistair said.

The two mice agreed that while they enjoyed their visits, they each liked their own house and lifestyle better.

"I'm going home to the good life," said Oliver as he shook his cousin's hand.

Oliver traveled back to the country and ate a supper of acorns and wheat kernels. Then he curled up under his oak leaves as he listened to the crickets chirp. He turned to his window and watched the fireflies flicker.

Back in the city, Alistair enjoyed the last of his pastry as he listened to the orchestra and watched ladies and gentlemen twirl around the bandstand.

Both of the mice sighed, and at the very same time they said, "I love being home."

HOM
SWE
HO

The Little Dutch Boy

Adapted by Regina Duffin
Illustrated by Linda Dockey Graves

Long ago there was a boy named Hans. He lived with his mother in a pretty little town in Holland. The land in Holland is very flat and lower than the sea. Dutch farmers had built high walls, called dikes, to keep the sea from flooding their farms and towns.

Like all Dutch children, little Hans knew that if a dike were to break, the fields would fill with seawater. The entire town would be flooded and ruined.

One day, Hans's mother packed a lunch basket for him to take to their friend, Mr. Van Notten. Hans knew that Mr. Van Notten lived far away and outside of town. Hans had walked there before and he knew that to walk there and back took a very long time.

Before Hans left, his mother reminded him to leave Mr. Van Notten's house with plenty of time to walk home before it grew dark.

On his way out of town, Hans followed the road that ran along the dike. After a while, he arrived at Mr. Van Notten's house.

Mr. Van Notten lived alone, and he was always glad when he had visitors. He also liked when Hans would come over with lunch.

Hans was quite hungry after his long walk, so Mr. Van Notten made cocoa and set out the bread and cheese that Hans's mother had sent. After their meal, the boy and the old man talked by the fire. They talked so long that neither of them paid attention to the time.

When Mr. Van Notten's dog scratched at the door to go outside, Hans noticed that the sky had become dark and stormy. He knew he had to head home quickly.

Hans could see that it was about to rain, so he started to walk home as fast as he could. He was not halfway home when the wind began to gust. A cold rain fell on Hans as he struggled against the wind. The weather made walking very difficult. "Just put one foot in front of the other," he told himself. "You will be home soon."

The strong wind made the trees bend low, and it flattened the flowers to the ground. Hans was quite cold by now, and he had to hold on to his hat to keep it from blowing away.

"I hope mother won't be upset when I arrive home so cold and wet and muddy," he thought.

Hans kept his head down against the wind as he trudged along the road. It was so dark that Hans didn't know where he was until he lifted his head and saw the dike in front of him. He knew that seeing the dike meant that he would be home very soon.

As Hans walked by the dike, he noticed that something was wrong. He could see a small hole in the wall allowing a trickle of water to seep through.

Hans knew immediately what must have happened. The storm had whipped up big waves in the sea on the other side of the dike. The pounding water had caused the wall to crack.

Hans knew he had to warn everyone in town that the dike had sprung a leak. The town was in great danger. Hans worried about his mother and the rest of his friends and family in the town.

He ran into town yelling, "The dike is breaking! Help! We must repair the dike!"

But no one heard him. All of the townspeople were snug in their homes. Every house and store in town was shut up tight against the storm. The doors were bolted, and the windows were shuttered.

Hans didn't give up. He called out again to the townspeople, warning them of the broken dike.

Still, no one answered.

Finally, Hans realized that no one could hear his cries.

He stopped running, caught his breath, and thought about what to do. He knew his mother must be worried about him, and he knew the crack in the dike was growing. Hans knew that the crack got bigger every minute, and it was only a matter of time before the sea would break through and wash away the town.

As fast as he could, Hans ran back to the place where he had seen the water seeping through the dike. Just like he thought, the crack had grown bigger.

Hans knew that the crack must be fixed right away. He wondered what he could possibly do to clog up the leak. After all his thinking, he could think of only one way to stop the leak.

Hans balled up his fist and pushed it into the hole to stop the seawater from pouring through.

Hans felt proud as he stood there, holding back the sea. He was sure that his mother would send people to look for him. But minutes turned into hours as Hans stood there, patiently protecting the dike and the town.

As darkness fell, Hans was getting cold and tired. His arm had begun to ache, and he had to force himself to remain standing.

He thought about the warmth of the fireplace at home as he stood in the cold rain by the dike. Then he thought about how good it would feel to lie down in his warm and dry bed.

As much as Hans wanted to set his arm down and head back home, he knew he had to save the town. He forced himself to stay awake and stay strong all through the night. It was all up to him.

When Hans did not come home that evening, his mother began to worry. As the rain fell, she kept watch, hoping Hans would return. Eventually, she decided that Hans must have stayed at Mr. Van Notten's house while he waited for the storm to pass.

Early the next morning, Mr. Van Notten walked to Hans's home. He wanted to thank Hans for his visit yesterday and thank his mother for the tasty food.

As Mr. Van Notten walked, he came upon Hans. The brave little boy was trembling and cold. Hans's arm hurt from the effort of keeping his fist wedged in the hole, and his legs were ready to collapse from standing all night. Still, Hans had to hold firm for just a little longer while Mr. Van Notten ran into town to alert the townspeople and find some help.

"Don't worry, Hans," said Mr. Van Notten. "I will be back as soon as I can find help. Just hang on a little longer."

Soon Mr. Van Notten returned with help. The townspeople began working to repair the dike as Mr. Van Notten wrapped Hans in blankets and carried him home to his mother. She put Hans to bed and gave him some warm broth to drink. Then she rubbed his fingers and his stiff legs to warm them up.

Word quickly spread through the town about how brave Hans had held back the sea all by himself. The townspeople were very curious. They went to the dike to see the hole that Hans had plugged.

As soon as Hans was warm and felt strong enough, he and his mother took a trip to the dike to see the repairs that were being made.

Everyone was overjoyed to see Hans. They gave him gifts fit for a hero. They shook his hand and marveled that he had been able to hold back the sea all by himself. Over and over, they thanked the boy for saving them.

Hans was very proud. He never imagined that he might one day save his town. His mother smiled down at him. She was very proud, too.

The town's mayor held a beautiful ceremony for Hans. He presented the boy with a medal in honor of the strength and courage he had shown in the face of grave danger. Everyone cheered loudly. They were all so proud of young Hans.

Hans smiled happily. He was honored to be thought of as a hero by everyone in the town.

Years later, after Hans had grown into a man, people continued to call him the little boy with the big heart.

The story of Hans and his bravery spread throughout all of Holland. To this day, the story of the courageous young boy has not been forgotten.

Rumpelstiltskin

Adapted by Maureen DuChamp
Illustrated by David Hohn

There once lived a poor miller who had nothing but his mill and his good daughter. More than anything, he wanted to give his daughter a happy and comfortable life.

One day, the miller had a chance to meet the king. Hoping to capture the king's attention, the miller boasted of his daughter. He spoke of her beauty and talent.

He said that she was also very smart and very kind. Furthermore, he claimed she could spin straw into gold!

The king was intrigued. The next day, he asked the miller's daughter to come to the palace. He showed her a room filled only with straw and a spinning wheel. He asked her to spin it all into gold by the next day.

The young woman had no idea how to spin gold from straw. At a loss for what to do, she began to cry. Suddenly, a little man appeared.

"Why are you crying?" he asked.

The young woman explained.

"I can spin this straw into gold for you," he said. "But if I help you, you must give me your necklace in return."

The miller's daughter agreed, and she handed him her necklace. It was the only thing of value that she owned, but she didn't know what else to do.

The little man set to work. Soon, the young woman fell asleep. When she awoke, the room was full of golden thread. The king was very pleased.

"This is a most remarkable talent you have," he said. "If you can repeat what you have done by tomorrow morning, I will make you my queen."

He showed her into another room, filled with even more straw. No sooner had the door closed than she began to cry.

Once again, the little man appeared to help.

"I will help you spin this straw into gold," he said. "But this time I will require something of greater value. You must promise me your firstborn child."

The woman hesitated. How could she make such a promise? But in her desperation, she agreed.

The odd little man set to work, and the young woman fell asleep. She awoke to find the straw spun into gold.

When the king arrived, he was amazed again. He asked her to be his queen.

"I will marry you on one condition," the young woman said. "You must promise never to ask me to spin straw into gold again."

The king agreed. Soon he and the miller's daughter were wed.

At first the new queen thought that her husband was a bit greedy. But she soon found him to be a sweet and caring man and a noble king. They grew to love each other.

A year after their wedding, their first child was born. The queen was so happy that she forgot all about her promise to the little man.

It was not until he appeared at her window one day that she remembered.

"Your Highness," said the odd man, "I have come to claim what is mine — your firstborn child. Your son belongs to me."

"Surely you will not take my child," said the queen. "I was a fool to make such a promise. Now that I am queen, I can give you anything you desire."

"What I desire is your child," he said. "You must keep your promise to me." He considered the queen as she cradled her child in her arms. Finally, he sighed. "I can see how much you love your son. If you can guess what my name is, I will forgive your promise."

"Horace?" the queen asked quickly. "Is your name Hubert? Hal?"

"Ha," he bellowed. "It is none of those. I will give you two more chances to guess."

With that, he turned and left the castle. The queen ordered one of her porters to follow him. The servant secretly watched the little man as he traveled deep into the forest. He set up camp, built a fire, and danced around it.

He knew the queen would never guess his name.

Meanwhile, the queen compiled a list. She sent for her royal advisers and asked them for the most unusual names they could find. They scoured the countryside and reported their findings to the queen.

The next day, the queen's porter returned to the castle. He had very little to report. The little man had danced around his fire all night long, but he did not speak a word.

Suddenly, a voice startled the queen.

"Have you any guesses for me, Your Highness?" asked the little man. He had appeared from out of nowhere.

"Indeed, I do," she said. "Are you called Monty? Mal? Montivecchio? Orton? Opyrus? Orenthal? Or perhaps you are Balthazar? Bitmillymont? Bugleheim?" The queen read every name from her list.

"All of your guesses are wrong!" said the little man triumphantly. "I will give you one more chance."

The queen returned to her list of names. She again asked her porter to follow the little man.

The porter found the little man in the same spot, deep in the forest. And just as he had the night before, the little man began to dance around his fire. This time, however, he sang a little song as he danced.

The queen's heart will surely break,
For tomorrow her child I'll take.
But now we play a guessing game,
And Rumpelstiltskin is my name!

The queen's porter smiled as he heard the mysterious name revealed. He made the long journey back to the palace, arriving only moments before the little man.

"It is time for your final guesses," said the little man.

The queen was ready for him this time.

"You do not look like an Alphonso or a Louie," said the queen. "Are you a Rumpelstiltskin?"

"That is impossible!" cried the man. "How could you know?"

In his fury, Rumpelstiltskin stomped his foot so hard on the floor that a hole opened up beneath him. He fell down into the hole and was never seen ever again.

The king and queen, their handsome little prince, and the miller lived happily ever after.

Demeter & Persephone

Adapted by Megan Musgrave
Illustrated by Mike Jaroszko

Hades, the king of the Underworld, sat on his lonely throne one day and wished that something could make his world a nicer place to live. The Underworld was cold and dark and dreary, and the sun never shined there. No one ever came to visit Hades because the gates of the Underworld were guarded by Cerberus, a huge dog with three heads. Cerberus looked so fierce that he scared everyone away.

It made Hades very upset to be the king of such a cold and lonely world. "I need a companion who will bring joy to this dark, dreary place," said Hades.

This gave Hades an idea. He decided to disguise himself as a poor, lonely traveler and go up to the earth's surface. There he would be able to find a companion. He would find someone who could help him make the Underworld a happier place to live.

Upon the earth lived Demeter, the goddess of the harvest. Demeter had a beautiful daughter named Persephone. Persephone had long, golden hair and rosy cheeks, and happiness followed her wherever she went. Demeter loved her daughter very much, and she was always full of joy when Persephone was near.

When the goddess of the harvest was happy, the whole world bloomed with life. The fields and orchards were always full of crops to be harvested.

Persephone loved to run through the fields and help Demeter gather food for the people of the earth. But best of all, she loved to play in the apple orchards.

When Hades was visiting the earth, he saw the goddess Persephone playing in an apple orchard. He had never seen such a beautiful girl!

Hades stood in his disguise at the edge of the orchard and watched Persephone as she swung on the branches.

Finally, Persephone saw Hades standing nearby. In his tattered cloak, he looked like a poor and hungry traveler. Persephone was always generous, so she picked several apples from the tree and climbed down to meet him.

"Please," said Persephone, "take these apples. They will give you strength for your journey."

Hades thanked Persephone for the apples and went on his way. "I must bring her to the Underworld!" he thought to himself. "It could never be a gloomy place with such a kind and beautiful queen as this!"

The next morning, Persephone decided to pick some apples. She began picking the ripest apples she could find.

Suddenly there was a great rumble, and the ground split open before her! Out from below the earth charged two fierce, black horses pulling a dark chariot behind them. On the chariot rode Hades, wearing the black armor of the Underworld.

Persephone tried to run away, but Hades was too quick for her. He caught her and took her away with him in his chariot to the Underworld. The ground closed back up behind them. Not a trace of Persephone was seen, except a few apples she left behind.

When Demeter came home from the fields, her daughter Persephone was nowhere to be seen. Demeter went to the orchard where Persephone had been picking apples, and found some apples spilled on the ground.

"Something terrible has to have happened to Persephone!" cried Demeter. She ran to search for her daughter. She decided to visit Helios, the god of the sun.

Helios sees everything on Earth. Demeter knew he must have seen what happened to her daughter.

"I have seen Persephone," Helios said. He told Demeter that Hades had taken Persephone to the Underworld to be his queen.

Demeter knew how unhappy Persephone would be in the Underworld. Demeter became sad and lonely for her daughter. The earth became cold and snowy, and the crops in the field faded and died.

In the Underworld, Persephone was sad and lonely, too. She tried to make her new home a more beautiful place, but nothing helped. The ground was too cold to plant seeds, and there was no sunshine to help them grow. Finally she asked Hades to let her return to the earth.

"But you are the queen of the Underworld!" exclaimed Hades. "Not many girls have the chance to be a queen. I am sure you will be happy here if you only stay a while longer."

Persephone became friends with Cerberus, who was lonely just like her. Sometimes he walked with her through the gloomy caves of the Underworld. But even with her new friend, Persephone missed the sunny days and lush fields back on the earth.

Demeter missed her daughter more and more each passing day. Finally she traveled to Mount Olympus, the home of the gods. She asked Zeus, the most powerful god of all, for his help.

"Hades has kidnapped my daughter Persephone and taken her to the Underworld to be his queen. Please help me bring her back to Earth again!" begged Demeter.

Zeus saw that the earth had become cold and barren. He knew that he had to help Demeter to make the earth fruitful again.

"I'll talk to Hades," said Zeus. "But I don't know if I can help her if she has eaten food from the Underworld."

Anyone who ate the food of the dead belonged forever to Hades. Zeus took his lightning bolt in hand and traveled to the Underworld.

"Hades!" thundered Zeus when he reached the gates of the Underworld. He made his way inside easily, for even fierce Cerberus was afraid of the king of the gods.

Zeus found Hades sitting sadly on his dark throne, watching Persephone. Persephone hardly looked like the beautiful girl she had been before. Her golden hair had grown dull, and her rosy cheeks were pale.

"Hades, I demand that you return Persephone to the earth," said Zeus. "Demeter misses her, and the earth has grown fruitless and barren since you stole her daughter."

"Very well," sighed Hades. "I thought her beauty would make my Underworld a happier place, but she is only sad and silent since she has come. You may take her back to the earth." But Hades did not want to lose his queen.

Hades was very clever, and he decided to trick Zeus and Persephone.

When Zeus was getting ready to take Persephone back to Earth, Hades took her aside for a moment.

"Here, take some food for your journey back to Earth," Hades said. Then he passed her a pomegranate, a fruit which has juicy seeds to eat.

Persephone thanked Hades for the food and ate just six pomegranate seeds. Then Zeus took Persephone back to the earth.

The pomegranate seeds that Persephone ate came from the Underworld. She had eaten them not knowing that eating food of the dead would keep her forever in that realm. Hades had tricked her.

When Persephone returned, Demeter was overjoyed. She was so happy to see her daughter that the earth bloomed again.

Suddenly, Hades appeared before them.

"Wait!" he exclaimed. "Persephone has eaten the food of the dead! She ate six seeds from a pomegranate before she came back to Earth. She must live in the Underworld with me forever!"

Zeus asked Persephone if this was true. She told Zeus how Hades had offered her those seeds for her journey back to Earth. Zeus was very angry about the trick Hades played on her.

He thought very carefully before he said, "Since you did eat six pomegranate seeds, you will spend one month of the year in the Underworld for each seed you ate. The other six months you will spend here on Earth."

And so each year when Persephone goes to the Underworld, her sad mother brings about the winter. But when Persephone returns in the spring, her mother is overjoyed and the seasons change again.

The Boy Who Cried Wolf

Adapted by Mary Rowitz
Illustrated by Jon Goodell

There was a young boy who lived in a village. He was a shepherd, and his job was to guard the sheep from danger, especially wolves.

Every day, in order to give the sheep the exercise they needed, the boy took them to a nearby valley. Once they had walked there, the sheep would graze on the tasty green grass that grew in the valley. The villagers trusted the shepherd to take good care of the sheep.

The village people worked nearby. If a wolf ever did attack, the people could run to the rescue.

The villagers trusted the shepherd boy to do his job. They never felt like they had to check on him.

Every day, the shepherd boy faithfully watched the sheep from his lookout post. He could also see the people hard at work in the village.

For the shepherd boy, every day was the same. He looked at the sheep. They looked the same every day. Then he looked out at the forest. It looked the same, too. While he was happy most days just to do his job, some days he wished that something exciting would happen.

One day the shepherd boy tried to make things more exciting. He thought, "Maybe I can play some games with the sheep." He planned his next day, and he smiled when he thought about the fun he would have.

The boy woke up bright and early the next morning. He ate his breakfast quickly and he kissed his parents good-bye. Then he hurried to take the sheep to the valley.

As soon as they reached the green grass in the valley, the boy tried to play games with the sheep.

The sheep, however, weren't interested. They didn't want to play any games with the shepherd boy. All the sheep wanted to do was eat the grass or take a nap. "This isn't any fun at all," thought the shepherd boy.

Downhearted, the shepherd boy walked slowly back to his lookout post. "I just wanted to make things a little more exciting around here," he thought to himself.

Then something in the forest caught the corner of his eye. "I wonder," he said, thinking out loud, "what is on the other side of those trees?" The boy smiled to himself. "Would it be so bad to pretend there was a wolf?" He thought this would be a good joke.

As the sheep ate the grass, he cupped his hand near his mouth and shouted, "Wolf! Wolf! A wolf is stealing the sheep! Come help me!"

All the village people stopped what they were doing and ran to help scare off the wolf.

When they got there, they were very confused.

The villagers didn't find a wolf. And where was the shepherd? They were worried about him. What if the wolf had stolen the boy? They frantically began to search high and low to find him.

Then one villager saw the boy and said, "There he is over there! Is he okay?" They saw he wasn't hurt at all. In fact, he was laughing!

"You looked so funny running up here for no reason. This was a great joke," laughed the boy.

The villagers did not laugh. They had been very scared for the boy and the sheep. They shook their heads and said, "We have to get back to work now. We don't have time for any silly pranks."

At breakfast the next day, the boy's mother and father told him to be good. He nodded his head and left to tend the sheep. Soon, however, he was bored again.

"Wolf! Wolf!" he shouted, louder than the day before. "A wolf is stealing the sheep! Come help me!"

Again the villagers came running. Again there was no wolf in sight. This time the village people were very upset. They told the boy, "If you don't tell people the truth all the time, they will never know when to believe you."

The boy was still laughing at his joke. After the villagers went back to their jobs, however, he started to think about what the people had said. "Maybe," he thought, "it isn't so funny to play tricks on others." The shepherd boy began walking back to his lookout post.

Just on the other side of the trees, a sly wolf had seen everything. When the shepherd boy reached his post, the wolf began stealing the sheep. The boy couldn't believe his eyes. It was a real wolf! He cried out, "Wolf! Wolf! A wolf is stealing the sheep! Come help me!"

He waited for the villagers, but no one came.

The boy yelled for help again, and still no one came.

He could only watch as the wolf ran off into the forest with all the sheep.

The shepherd boy ran into the village. "Wolf! Wolf!" he cried. "He's stealing our sheep!" The boy kept running and calling for help, but no one believed he was telling the truth. He called out again, "Wolf! Wolf!"

"I bet!" said one villager. "I can't believe that boy is trying to make fools out of us again."

"Well, he's not going to make a fool out of me," said another villager. "I don't believe him."

Finally the shepherd boy stopped running. "I'm telling the truth this time," he said. "There really is a wolf in the valley, and he's stealing the sheep. You've got to believe me."

The villagers came and looked at the boy. They shook their fingers at him. "We're smarter than you think," the people said. "This time we're just going to ignore you!"

At that moment, the shepherd boy knew no one would believe him. How could he blame them? When they trusted him, he let them down. He lost their trust by not always telling the truth.

He sadly walked back to his lookout and gazed down where he always took his sheep to eat grass. But there weren't any sheep left. The wolf had taken all of them away. The boy was so sad that he began to cry.

The boy remembered what his parents and the villagers had told him. How he wished he had listened to what they said. He wished he had never made up that lie about the wolf for fun. He wished he had always told the truth and that the sheep would be safe.

Because he didn't tell the truth, no one believed him when it really mattered. Now it was too late. The shepherd boy didn't think his joke was so funny anymore.

Rip Van Winkle

Adapted by Brian Conway
Illustrated by John Lund

The Catskill Mountains are magical. They are a wild place, filled with many beautiful sights. Clear brooks run down the hills. Valleys spread out wide. Stone cliffs rise up to the sky. Tall trees reach into the clouds.

The mountain people tell legends of amazing stories. They seem too strange to be true but one can never be sure.

One story is about a man named Rip Van Winkle.

Rip lived in a town in the foothills. He was a friendly man. He always had a smile for anyone he met. He greeted everybody with a tip of his hat and everyone loved him.

The children in town especially loved him. Rip always played games with them. He flew kites, shot marbles and even jumped rope with them.

Even the neighborhood dogs loved Rip. They never barked when he passed by.

Rip Van Winkle was a wonderful neighbor. He could never turn down a neighbor who asked for help. He always helped his neighbors with their chores.

Rip had just one fault. He never did his own chores.

His fences always fell over. The weeds in his yard always grew fast and wild. His cow was always running away. His pigs were always trampling through the garden.

Rip's children were as raggedy as his farm. Their clothes were always torn. Their faces were always dirty. They ran around without shoes. They did not like to do their chores either.

Rip and his dog Wolf spent a lot of time in the mountains. Rip liked to go fishing. Wolf liked to hunt for rabbits and squirrels.

Some days, they just walked through the foothills.

"I have had a busy day," Rip said.

Wolf wagged his tail as Rip petted him.

"Let's find a place where there are no fences," he said.

They walked up one of the mountains. Halfway up, Rip sat down and enjoyed the view. Wolf sat next to him.

Rip and Wolf passed the whole afternoon that way.

"It's getting late," Rip said. "We should get home."

"Rip Van Winkle," a voice said.

Rip turned around. He saw a strange little man. He carried a huge barrel on his shoulder.

"Would you help me with this?" the little man asked.

The little man was strange. But Rip could not refuse anyone who asked for help.

"Of course," Rip said. "I would love to help."

He took the barrel from the strange little man. He climbed up the mountain with him.

He led Rip and Wolf through a crack in a cliff.

Inside, there was a clearing.

There was a group in the clearing. Many strange little men were gathered there. Rip stared at them.

"Thank you, neighbor," one strange little man said.

He took the barrel from Rip. He poured a dark liquid from it. The strange little men passed around cups and drank the strange liquid.

They offered a cup to Rip. He drank the dark liquid. It was very tasty. He asked for more.

He drank several cups and started to feel tired. His eyes drooped. His head felt heavy. He drifted off to sleep.

It was morning when Rip woke up. The sun was shining high in the sky. It was almost noon.

He was no longer in the clearing. He was back where he had first met the little man.

"I have been here all night," he said. "Mrs. Van Winkle is going to be very upset with me."

He whistled for his dog. Wolf did not come running.

"Maybe Wolf ran home," he said.

Rip's knees cracked when he stood up.

"Sleeping outside isn't good for me," he said. "My legs feel like they belong to an old man."

He started down the hill.

He had dreamed about strange little men. He remembered his dream as he walked. The dream had seemed so real. He felt confused.

Rip walked into town. The people he saw did not look familiar. He did not know anyone. They did not seem to know him.

The townspeople stared at Rip. He smiled. He waved. He tipped his hat. Some of the people laughed. Others looked the other way.

Finally, Rip looked down. He saw why everyone had been staring at him. He had a long gray beard!

Rip's beard had grown down to his knees. It was gray and white. It was knotted and tangled.

His clothes were ripped and tattered. He was dirty.

Children raced up to Rip.

"Who are you, old man?" one boy asked.

"What are you doing in our town?" asked another.

Rip was more confused than ever.

He walked through town. The people were different. The buildings were different. The dogs barked at him.

"I'd better get home," Rip said.

But Rip got lost on the way to his house. The paths and roads were no longer the same.

After some time, Rip found his farmhouse. It did not look at all like it had the day before. The fence had fallen to the ground. Weeds grew all over. The roof was falling in. The front door was swinging on its hinges.

Rip waited for his wife and children to appear.

No one moved around the house. No one came out.

Rip walked slowly toward the house. It was dark and dirty inside. Nobody had lived there in a very long time.

Rip ran back to town. He wanted to find something familiar or someone who remembered him.

A man dressed in a fine suit walked up to Rip.

"What are you doing here?" he asked.

"I am looking for someone who remembers me," Rip told the man.

Then a woman and her family walked up to Rip. They wanted to meet the old, bearded stranger.

"Hello," the woman said. "I am Judith Gardener. These are my children."

The children were afraid of the stranger. Rip leaned forward to look at Judith's face.

"What is your father's name?" he asked.

"Rip Van Winkle was his name," she said.

"What became of him?" Rip asked.

"He walked up into the mountains one day," she said. "He never came back. His dog came home without him. We have not heard anything about him since."

"And what about your mother?" Rip asked.

"She passed away a few months ago," Judith said.

Rip began to cry. His wife was gone. His children had grown. He had missed twenty years of his life!

"Are you all right, sir?" Judith asked.

"Don't you recognize me?" Rip asked. "I'm your father!"

Judith looked into old Rip's eyes and knew it was him. Rip hugged his daughter and told his family about the little men. He told them about the clearing in the mountains and the liquid he drank.

The whole town gathered to hear Rip's story. Everyone was glad to have old Rip Van Winkle back.

His story became a legend.

The Little Red Hen

Adapted by Jennifer Boudart
Illustrated by Linda Dockey Graves

Once there was a little red hen who had five little chicks. They lived on a farm with their good friends the dog, the cat, and the duck.

One day while sweeping the yard, the little red hen found some kernels of wheat on the ground. She put the kernels into her pocket and went to look for the dog, cat, and duck.

"Will you help me plant seeds?" she asked.

The three friends looked at each other. "Heavens, no!" they chuckled.

"Then I'll plant the seeds myself," she told them. So the little red hen went straight to the field and began digging.

Soon her baby chicks came to see what their mother was doing.

"Can we help you, Mother?" asked one of her chicks.

The little red hen was delighted that all of her chicks wanted to help. Together they pretended that they were burying little treasures across the field as they planted each seed. The game made their work go quickly, and all of the kernels of wheat were planted in the field that day.

The little red hen and her chicks visited their plants every day. They checked each little treasure they had planted to make sure they were getting plenty of sunshine and care.

The dog, the cat, and the duck watched the little red hen and her chicks tend to their plants.

"That looks exhausting!" they exclaimed.

One day the little red hen found her three friends leaning against the farmer's barn.

"There are weeds in the wheat patch," she said. "Will you help me pull them up?"

"I can't," said the cat. "They're so dirty, and it would take too long to clean my paws afterwards."

"My leg hurts," said the dog. "So I won't be able to help you either."

"I have to go swimming," said the duck as he waddled away in the water.

"I'll do it myself," said the little red hen as she walked back to the field with her chicks. They started a contest to see who could pull the most weeds. The chicks had such a wonderful time that they were finished pulling weeds in no time at all.

The cat, the dog, and the duck all watched as the little birds worked. "It's much too fine outside to worry about silly weeds," said the cat.

"I'd rather sit in the shade," said the dog.

The little red hen knew she must water her wheat so that it would grow tall and strong. She went looking for her friends, who were resting on the porch. The hen said, "Who will help me water my wheat?"

The dog, the cat, and the duck rolled their eyes at the little red hen.

"I'm busy making up a song," growled the dog. "Don't you hear my banjo?"

"I'm busy thinking up the words," said the cat. "Don't you see my pencil and paper?"

"I'm busy playing the beat," said the duck. "Don't you see my drum?"

"I'll just water the wheat myself," said the little red hen. So she took her watering can to the garden.

Her chicks came along to help. The hen pretended to be a thundercloud and sprinkled the chicks with water. Before long, all of the wheat had been watered.

The wheat grew fast in the summer sun. Soon it was fall and the wheat turned golden brown. The little red hen knew what that meant. She found her friends playing cards under the farmer's wagon. The hen knelt down and said, "Who will help me harvest the wheat?"

The dog, the cat, and the duck kept their eyes on their cards. "Not us!" they said. "Can't you see we're busy?"

"I'll harvest it myself," said the little red hen. So the little red hen and her chicks went into the field to harvest the wheat and tie it into bundles. They sang songs and played games until the hard work was done.

"Look at that silly red hen," said the dog. "She's grown so much wheat, she won't know what to do with it all."

"All of that hard work to make more hard work!" said the duck, nodding in disapproval.

"Who will help me carry the wheat to the miller?" asked the little red hen.

It was time for the wheat to be ground into flour.

The dog, the cat, and the duck couldn't imagine doing such hard work on such a beautiful fall day.

"Not me," said the dog. "I'm busy playing a fun game of chess."

"Not me," said the cat. "I'm in the middle of a long and beautiful catnap."

"Not me," said the duck. "I need to fluff my feathers in the sun."

The little red hen and her chicks would have to do it themselves. The trip to the miller went very fast. The hen and the chicks pretended to be fearless explorers on an uncharted path.

On the way home, they thought of all the delicious things they could make with their fresh wheat.

The next day the hen and the chicks went to the mill to pick up the wheat, which had been ground into flour.

When they returned home, the little red hen called out, "Who will help me bake bread with my flour?"

The dog and the cat didn't bother answering.

"All of that work isn't worth a loaf of bread!" said the duck to his friends.

"I'll bake it myself," said the hen. So the little red hen and her five chicks mixed and kneaded and baked their flour into a lovely loaf of bread. While the bread baked in the oven, all of the little chicks helped clean up the kitchen.

They pretended the bowls, spoons, and cups were delicate seashells as they washed each one and gently put them away. Next they danced and sang together as they swept the floor with their little wings.

Soon the smell of baking bread floated into the air. The dog, the cat, and the duck peeped into the kitchen.

"Who is going to help me eat this bread?" asked the little red hen.

"We will!" cried the dog, cat, and duck.

"Did you help plant seeds?" asked the hen.

"No," answered her friends.

"Did you help weed the field?" asked the hen.

"No," answered her friends.

"Did you help water, or harvest, or carry the wheat?" asked the hen.

"Well, no," answered her friends.

"Did you help make bread? Or clean up the kitchen?" asked the hen.

Her friends shook their heads.

"You can only have a piece of my bread if you helped me grow it, carry it, or bake it," said the little red hen.

That night, the hen and her chicks filled their tummies with fresh bread to reward all of their hard work.

The dog, the cat, and the duck who didn't help at all got none.

Three Billy Goats Gruff

Adapted by Carolyn Quattrocki
Illustrated by Tim Ellis

Once there were three Billy Goats Gruff. The oldest was Big Billy Goat Gruff, who wore a collar of thick black leather. Middle Billy Goat Gruff had a red collar around his neck, and Little Billy Goat Gruff wore a yellow collar on his neck.

Big Billy Goat Gruff had a deep, gruff billy goat voice. Middle Billy Goat Gruff had a middle-sized billy goat voice. And Little Billy Goat Gruff had a very high, little billy goat voice.

All winter long, the three Billy Goats Gruff lived on a rocky hillside. They loved to run and jump and play.

Next to their hill ran a powerful, rushing river.

Every day during the cold winter months, the three Billy Goats Gruff played among the rocks.

Big Billy Goat Gruff was the best climber and the strongest of the three billy goats. He had strong legs and big, curved horns. Big Billy Goat Gruff was also the smartest of the three billy goats. Whenever there was a problem, Big Billy Goat Gruff was always the one to find a solution.

Middle Billy Goat Gruff and Little Billy Goat Gruff would have fun watching Big Billy Goat Gruff jump over the biggest rocks and the steepest ravines. They liked to challenge the big goat to see what he could do. Big Billy Goat Gruff liked the challenges because they made him feel bigger and mightier than even the mountain range.

At night the wind would blow coldly over the three Billy Goats Gruff.

Little Billy Goat Gruff looked up to see a sky filled with bright, shining stars.

Middle Billy Goat Gruff looked up at the night to see the thin sliver of a winter moon.

Big Billy Goat Gruff said, "Enough looking at the sky, it is time to find a place to sleep."

So the three Billy Goats Gruff found a nice, cozy cave to sleep in for the night.

Sometimes, when Little Billy Goat Gruff could not sleep, Big Billy Goat Gruff made shadows on the cave wall. Not only was Big Billy Goat Gruff big and tough, but he had a big heart, too.

Soon it was springtime. From their rocky hillside the three Billy Goats Gruff looked longingly across the rushing river to the meadow.

"How I would love to go up the mountain across the river," said Little Billy Goat Gruff.

"To get to the mountain," said Middle Billy Goat Gruff, "we will have to cross the bridge over the river."

The three Billy Goats Gruff knew that under the bridge lived a mean, ugly troll. The troll had eyes that were as big as saucers, a head of shaggy hair, and a nose that was as long as a broomstick.

The evil troll always said that he would eat any billy goats that tried to cross the bridge. He was a nasty troll.

"You two can't go across the bridge," said Big Billy Goat Gruff. "It isn't safe." He was always looking out for the other two billy goats.

So the three Billy Goats Gruff stayed on their rocky side of the river and played and jumped. They had many animal friends on their side of the river that were also too afraid to cross the bridge. Still, they wanted to see what was on the other side.

Every day the Billy Goats Gruff looked across the river.

"The grass looks so sweet over there," said Little Billy Goat Gruff. "Let's go over the bridge."

"The flowers smell like honey!" said Middle Billy Goat Gruff. "Yes, let's go over the bridge."

"But what are we to do about the evil troll?" asked Big Billy Goat Gruff.

One day, as they were looking at the green mountain, Big Billy Goat Gruff had an idea. He thought of a plan to trick the troll so that they could cross the bridge and go to the other side.

The next morning the three Billy Goats Gruff went down to the river. Little Billy Goat Gruff started to cross the bridge.

Trip-trap, trip-trap, trip-trap, went Little Billy Goat Gruff's feet on the bridge.

"Who's that trip-trapping across my bridge?" roared the troll.

"It is only I, Little Billy Goat Gruff," said Little Billy Goat Gruff quietly.

"I'm coming to eat you up!" said the troll.

"Oh, no!" said Little Billy Goat Gruff. "I am only a tiny, little billy goat. Wait for my brother, Middle Billy Goat Gruff. He will make a much bigger meal for you."

So the troll let Little Billy Goat Gruff cross the bridge to the other side. Then the troll patiently waited for Middle Billy Goat Gruff to come trip-trapping across the bridge. The troll was quite hungry, but decided he could wait for the middle goat.

In a little while, Middle Billy Goat Gruff started across the wooden bridge.

Trip-trap, trip-trap, trip-trap, went Middle Billy Goat Gruff's feet.

"Who's that trip-trapping across my bridge?" roared the troll.

"It is only I, Middle Billy Goat Gruff," he said.

"I'm coming to eat you up!" said the troll.

"Oh, no!" said Middle Billy Goat Gruff loudly. "I'm only a middle-sized billy goat. Wait for my brother, Big Billy Goat Gruff. He will make a much bigger dinner."

The troll let Middle Billy Goat Gruff cross the bridge.

Finally Big Billy Goat Gruff walked on the bridge.

TRIP-TRAP, TRIP-TRAP, TRIP-TRAP, went Big Billy Goat Gruff as he walked on the bridge.

"Who's TRIP-TRAPPING across my bridge?" roared the troll.

"It is I, Big Billy Goat Gruff," he said.

"I'm coming to eat you up!" said the troll. Then Big Billy Goat Gruff, with his two big horns, tossed the troll high into the air, and he fell down into the river below.

The troll was gone! All the animals were now free to cross the bridge without fear.

The three Billy Goats Gruff were happy to be on the other side. They feasted on the green grass and the wildflowers in the field.

"I was right," said Little Billy Goat Gruff. "The grass tastes as sweet as it smells."

"And I was right, too," said Middle Billy Goat Gruff. "The flowers taste like honey."

"Best of all, I was right," said Big Billy Goat Gruff. "We were able to trick the evil troll and cross the bridge."

So the three Billy Goats Gruff spent their summer happily eating in the high meadows.

The three Billy Goats Gruff could run and jump and play tag in the open meadow.

But whether they were playing their games amongst the rocks or tag in the meadow, they knew they were safe.

The troll was never seen again.

The Four Musicians

Adapted by Mary Rowitz
Illustrated by Wendy Edelson

One day a donkey was walking along the fence by the barn, singing softly to himself. He stopped when he heard his owner talking with another farmer. The donkey leaned in closer so he could better hear the conversation.

"I know what you mean," one farmer said. "Sometimes it's easier to just get a younger one."

The donkey wondered what they could be talking about, and he leaned in even closer.

His owner continued, "I just can't find many reasons to keep the tired bag of bones around much longer. He is very old and cannot pull the plow anymore. It's time to put that old donkey out to pasture."

The donkey couldn't believe his ears! They were talking about him! He was very hurt to hear these words.

"Hee-haw!" said the donkey. "I won't be sent out to pasture. I'll go to the town of Bremen and become a famous musician."

The donkey had just started on his way when he saw a sad dog sitting by the road. The donkey asked what was bothering the dog.

"My owner says I am too old to hunt," howled the dog. "He wants to get a younger dog who keeps quiet."

"I have an idea," said the donkey. "Why don't you come with me to Bremen, and we will work as musicians. We'll be quite a pair."

"Woof!" said the dog. "I really like that idea!" The two new pals had not gone far before they crossed paths with a gloomy cat. They asked what was wrong.

"My owner says I am too old," said the cat.

"He wants to get a younger cat who can catch mice better," the cat continued to cry.

They invited the cat to come to Bremen to sing with them. "Mee-ow!" answered the cat, and the three were on their way.

The dog, cat, and donkey were walking along when suddenly a very upset rooster flew right into the middle of the road. "Cock-a-doodle-day!" the rooster squawked.

"What a strong voice you have!" the dog said.

"My owners say there is no point in having a strong voice if you don't use it every day," crowed the rooster. "I cannot get up early enough to wake up the workers anymore. My owners plan to serve me for Sunday dinner!"

"Join us on our trip," said the dog. "We are going to work as musicians. We could really use your strong voice to make our band complete."

"Cock-a-doodle-day!" said the rooster.

The four new friends practiced singing as they walked toward Bremen.

Nighttime came. The donkey, dog, cat, and rooster had been singing and walking all day. Just when the four musicians found a nice tree to camp under, the rooster began to squawk. "I think I see a light shining from inside a house!" he said. "It doesn't seem far away."

"They might have some food to share," said the dog. "A big, juicy bone sounds mighty good right about now."

"Mmmm. I think a big bowl of milk would be absolutely purr-fect," purred the cat.

"A plate of corn certainly would hit the spot," crowed the rooster. The donkey thought it all sounded good, so the four set out for the house.

The four musicians walked up to the house. The donkey, being the tallest of the group, reached his head up and peered inside the window.

After the donkey had looked through the glass for a few moments, the cat's curiosity got the better of him.

"What do you see?" he asked as he tried to get a glimpse himself.

"Well, there are four men sitting at a table that is covered with food," the donkey said. "They must eat like this every night. There are stacks of gold everywhere, perhaps they are kings of some kind."

"What do we do now?" asked the rooster. "Do we just knock on the door and ask for food?"

The donkey shook his head. "Remember we are going to be musicians," he said. "We should practice singing for our supper." The others thought this was a great idea.

The four friends didn't know that the men inside were robbers. They were hiding out in that house and counting gold they had stolen.

The friends got ready for their first concert.

The four musicians decided to stand one on top of the other so everyone could be heard. First the donkey took his place near the bottom of the window. Then the dog jumped on his back. The cat made his way up to the dog's back. Finally the rooster flew to the top.

Even though the four friends had practiced their singing all day, they were still nervous. This was their first concert, after all. They wished each other good luck, turned to face the window, and cleared their throats. Finally their big moment had arrived. It was time to perform. The donkey gave the signal, and they began to sing.

Never had there been a louder or mightier group effort! The four friends tried to sing better than they ever had before.

However, what they didn't know is that it didn't sound like singing. It sounded like, "Hee-haw! Woof! Mee-ow! Cock-a-doodle-day!"

When the robbers heard the loud noise, they looked out the window. They saw what looked like a four-headed beast. "Run! Run! Run!" one robber yelled. "Run before the four-headed beast gets us!" The robbers ran out of the house in terror.

The animals were confused. Why had the men run away? The donkey said, "I think I know what has happened. No doubt that they enjoyed our singing so much that they must be going to get more people to hear our concert."

"It may be some time before they return with a bigger audience," the rooster said. "I say we go inside and have ourselves some of that dinner as a reward for our splendid singing."

"Indeed!" agreed the donkey. "That is a great idea!"

The four musicians went into the house and made themselves comfortable.

They sat together around the table and feasted. The four musicians were so hungry that they ate every last bite! It didn't take long to decide that the life of a musician was going to suit them very well indeed.

Soon after the meal, they were very sleepy. Since they were already inside the house, they agreed it would be best to spend the night there. After all, they didn't want to miss the people who were going to come hear them perform.

There was plenty of room for everyone in the house. The donkey lay in the middle of the room. The dog stretched out by the door. The cat curled up near the fireplace, and the rooster flew to a ceiling beam.

Soon their sleepy heads began nodding. It didn't take long for their tired eyes to close. They were all sound asleep when the door knob slowly began to turn. They were still asleep when someone tiptoed into the room.

It was one of the robbers coming back.

He had returned to see if he could get some of the gold back. It was quite dark, and he needed some light in order to find his way around. He thought he saw a glow from the coals in the fireplace. But the glow wasn't from the coals. It was the cat's eyes. When he lit a match to start a fire, the cat jumped up. The robber tripped over the dog. The dog bit his leg, causing the robber to stumble over the donkey. The donkey kicked the robber. The noise woke the rooster, and he began crowing, "Cock-a-doodle-day! Leave without delay!"

The robber ran as fast as his legs would carry him. He told the other robbers to stay away from that house forever or the four-headed beast would get them.

The four musicians lived in the house for the rest of their days. They were quite happy giving free concerts to anyone who visited. And there was enough gold there to pay for all the food they would ever need.

The End

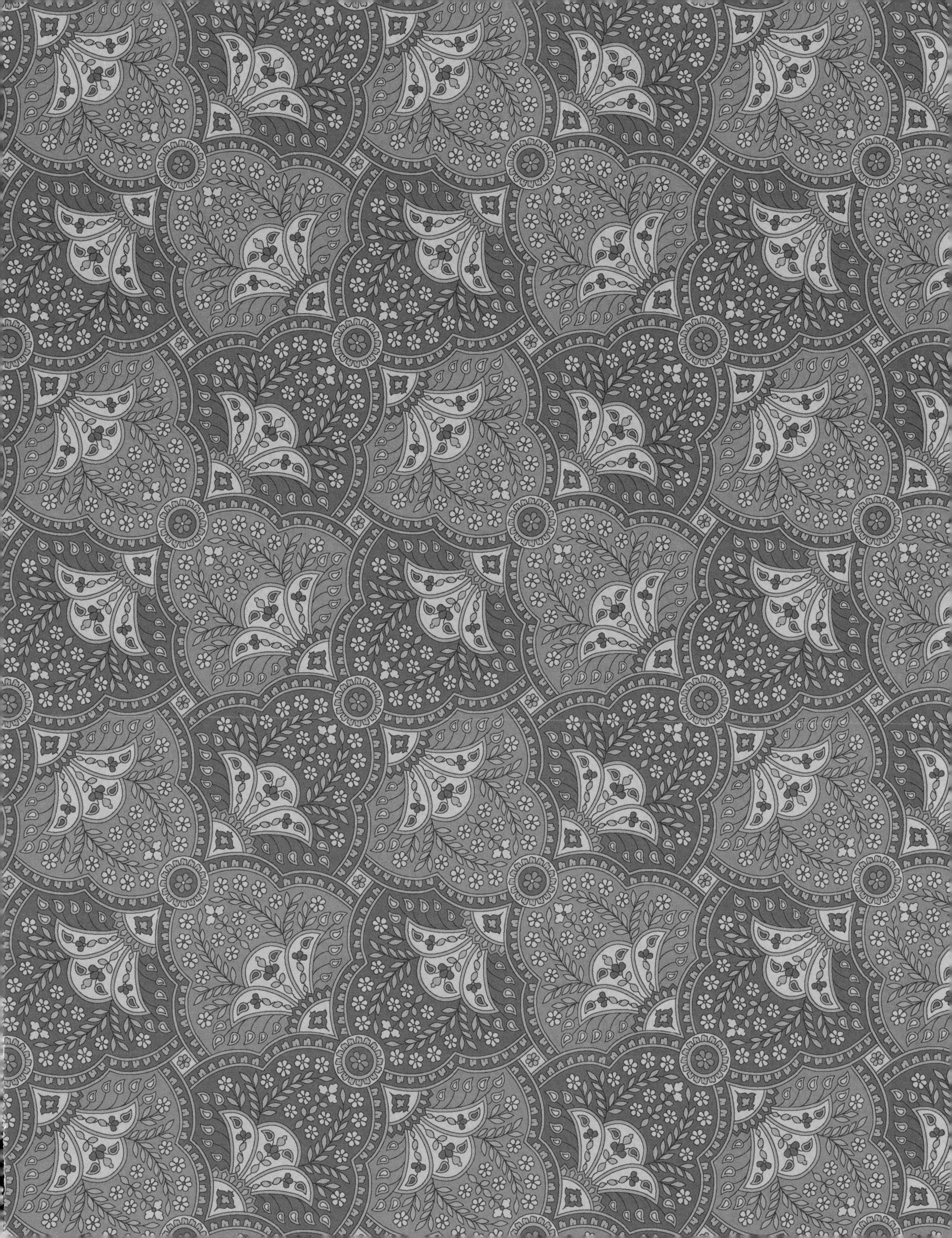